This Little Tiger book belongs to:

_____

_____

_____

Duck panicking.

Fox is ready to eat.!!

Duck surprised

Fox ready to pounce -

Fox's hair stands on end !!

Fox looks sad and sorry for himself -

Scat?

With much love to Helen and Ray — C F

For Lou, Finn & Tilly, love — N E

VIXEN ♦ PERFUME

A. HOGG & SON

City Farm

LITTLE TIGER PRESS
1 The Coda Centre, 189 Munster Road, London SW6 6AW
www.littletigerpress.com
First published in Great Britain 2012
This edition published 2012

Text copyright © Claire Freedman 2012 • Illustrations copyright © Nick East 2012
Claire Freedman and Nick East have asserted their rights to be identified as the
author and illustrator of this work under the Copyright, Designs and Patents Act, 1988
A CIP catalogue record for this book is available from the British Library
All rights reserved • ISBN 978-1-84895-488-5 • Printed in China
LTP/1400/0576/0213 • 10 9 8 7 6 5 4 3 2

Who's For DINNER?

Claire Freedman * Nick East

LITTLE TIGER PRESS
London

On a friendly little farm, in the middle
of the countryside, lived Hen, Duck, Lamb and Bull.
All their days were hap-hap-happy,
UNTIL . . .

. . . one day, a hungry **City Fox** came prowling.

"Oooh, this must be a **farm**," cried Fox.

"At **last**! Hurrah! I bet it's full of plump

uicy, DELICIOUS animals. All for me!

Hee hee!"

"Oh HELP!" squawked Hen, and she flapped home to warn her friends.

"We'll be fox food by teatime!" Hen cried.

"We're done for!" trembled Lamb.

"Don't panic!" said Bull.

"It's alright for you! You won't get eaten!" snapped Duck.

"No one will – if we're clever!" smiled Bull.
"We can easily out-fox that City Fox."

And Bull explained his wild and crazy plan.

A little later, Hen was sitting in the sunshine when Fox appeared.

"Ooh! Goody-goody!" he drooled. "You look like a tasty treat! Get ready to be gobbled up!"

"But you can't eat *me*," said Hen, shaking her coconut hooves at Fox. "I'm a horse! Foxes don't eat horses!"

"NEIGH!" she clucked.

"NEIGH! NEIGH! NEIGH!"

"A horse!" gasped Fox in surprise.
"You? Really?" And he flicked through
his book crossly.

"Pointy ears, long tail,
DO NOT EAT!"

HORSE

Pointy
ears

Long
tail

DO
NOT
EAT!

"Hmph! I'll have to find something
else to munch!" And growling grumpily,
Fox prowled on . . .

. . . straight to Duck's pond. Fox smiled slyly,
opened his wide, slobbering jaws
and pounced!

"Hello dinner!"
he cackled.

Duck's
Pond

"I'm not your dinner!" said Duck crossly.
"I'm a COW! Everyone knows foxes
don't eat cows!"

"MOOOOOO

he quacked.

"Mooo!
Mooo!
Moo

"A COW?!" Fox snapped back. "You're a

COW?!"

He flipped through his book angrily.

"Horns,
    patches,
        bell,
            DO NOT EAT!"

"HMPH!
Here's me almost **fainting** with hunger and all I find is a useless COW!"
Fox kicked some stones, and stamped on a daisy. Then he stomped off . . .

. . . and found a tasty-looking lamb.
Fox eyed up Lamb hungrily
and licked his lips.
"Dinner time!" he growled.

donkey
rescue

"Goodness, you can't eat me!"
Lamb squeaked. "I'm a d-d-donkey!
Foxes don't eat donkeys.
Hee-Haw!" she bleated.

free
donkey
rides

"Hee-Haw!
Hee-Haw!
Hee-Haw!"

"A **donkey?**" roared Fox.
"This is **terrible!**
I'm **dying** with hunger!"

Fox thundered off in a wild rage all the way
to the hen-house. In a terrifying fury,
he **threw** the door open,
and found . . .

eggs
for
sale

"Aa-aagh!" cried Fox.
"You're GI-GI-NORMOUS!
What are you?"

"I am a chicken!"
said Bull. "Can't you see?
CLUCK!" he snorted.

"CLUCK!
CLUCK!
CLUCK!"

Fox trembled in terror.
"You? A ch-ch-chicken?" he whimpered.
"But I thought foxes were meant
to EAT chickens!"

Bull snorted and pointed his huge horns
right at Fox.

"If foxes EAT chickens,"
he bellowed . . .

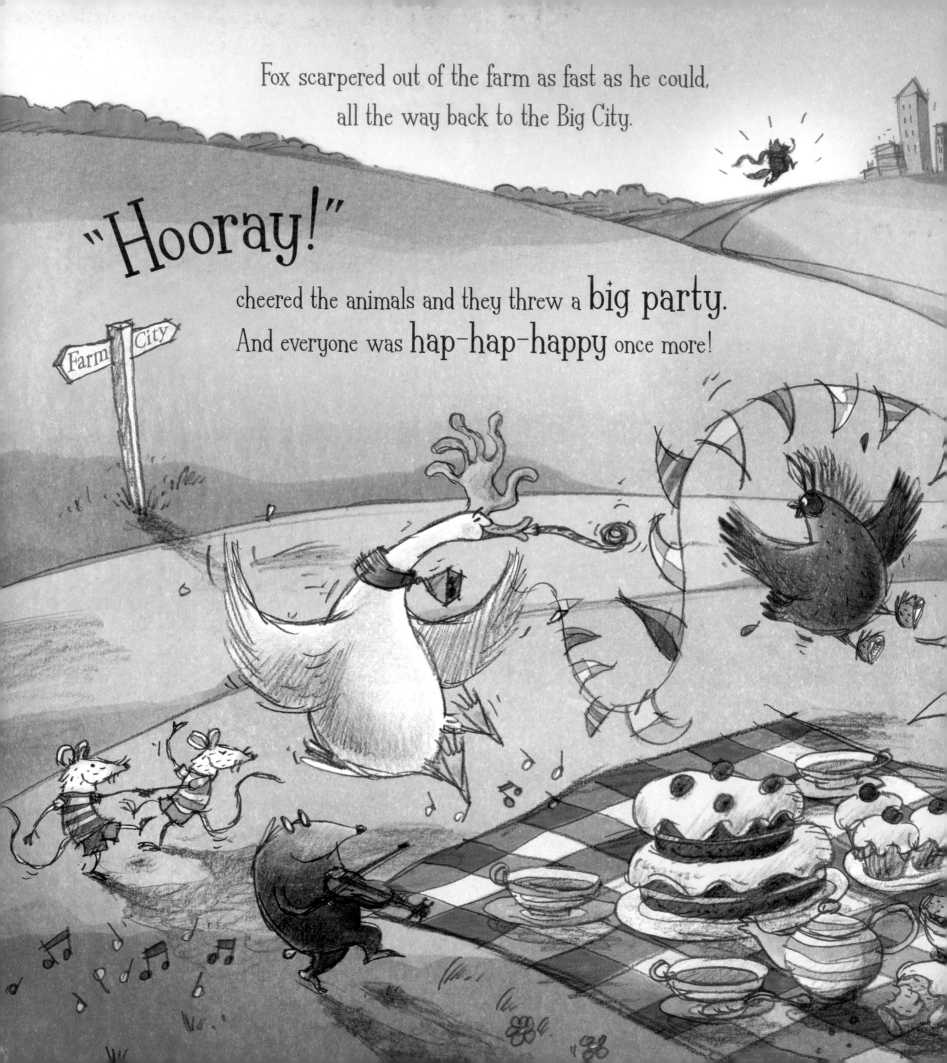

Fox scarpered out of the farm as fast as he could,
all the way back to the Big City.

"Hooray!"

cheered the animals and they threw a big party.
And everyone was hap-hap-happy once more!

Farm City

Duck panicking.

Fox is ready to eat!!

Duck surprised.

Fox ready to pounce.

Fox's hair stands on end!!

Fox looks sad and sorry for himself.

Scarf?

More yummy books from Little Tiger Press!

For information regarding any of the above titles
or for our catalogue, please contact us:
Little Tiger Press, 1 The Coda Centre,
189 Munster Road, London SW6 6AW
Tel: 020 7385 6333 • Fax: 020 7385 7333
E-mail: info@littletiger.co.uk • www.littletigerpress.com